HAPPY BIRTHDAY × 3

LIBBY GLEESON

ILLUSTRATED BY

For my three
L.G.

For Bridie Murphy
D.C.

First published 2007 by Walker Books Ltd
87 Vauxhall Walk, London SE11 5HJ

6 8 10 9 7 5

Text © 2007 Libby Gleeson
Illustrations © 2007 David Cox

The right of Libby Gleeson and David Cox to be identified as author and illustrator respectively of this work has been asserted by them in accordance with the Copyright, Designs and Patents Act 1988

This book has been typeset in Bembo Educational
and Tempus Sans ITC

Printed and bound in China

British Library Cataloguing in Publication Data:
a catalogue record for this book is available from the British Library

ISBN: 978-1-4063-0428-2

www.walker.co.uk

Earning Some Money

"Mum," said Amy at breakfast, "you know how it's our birthday next week…"

"How could I forget?" said Mum. "Triplets' birthday. Three cakes, three lots of presents…"

"Three times the fun," said Josephine.

That was how Mum always
answered when people looked at
the girls, shook their heads and said,
"Three times the work."

"Three times the fun," said Mum.

 "I need to
buy presents
for Jo and Jess,"
said Amy.

"And I need
to buy presents
for Jess and Amy,"
said Jo.

 "Me too," said
Jess. "I need to
buy presents for
Amy and Jo."

"Have you got any money?" said Mum.

"No."   "No."   "No."

"Well, you'll have to make something special for each other, then."

The girls shook their heads.

"We want to buy presents."

"We can earn some money."

"We can do jobs."

"Last year," said Jess, "we made cakes for each other."

"And another time," said Jo, "we painted pictures for each other."

"This year," said Amy, "Dad said if we did real jobs we would get some money."

Mum thought for a minute. "Well, your room's a big mess…" She looked at each of the girls in turn. "It needs a clean-up. And I mean a *really* good clean."

Mum opened the door to the bedroom.
Books. Clothes. Toys.
Toys. Clothes. Books.
Everywhere you looked, there were
more clothes, more books and more toys.

"By lunchtime I want this room
spotless. OK?"

"OK, Mum."

"I want the books stacked neatly in
the bookshelf, the toys in the toy box
and the clothes in the cupboards.
You've got a lot to do this morning!
I'll see you in
a few hours."

Amy, Jo and Jess sat in the middle
of the bedroom.

"This won't take long," said Amy
and she picked up a spinning top
and flicked it, spinning,
under the bunk.

"No," said Jo as she opened a book
about monsters and began to read.

Jess had pulled off her top
and was trying on one
of Jo's that she had
found under the
wardrobe.

All morning they played. Amy found the fire engine that she had thought they'd lost. She built a town with the construction set and tried to work out which building she could burn down. Jo finished her book on monsters but found another one about dinosaurs, and she wondered which one sounded scarier: Tyrannosaurus or Triceratops.

Jess took off her
jeans to see whether
the stripy skirt
or the one
with spots on
looked better with
the white T-shirt.

Amy made a hurricane knock over
her whole town and then she played
a game of cards against the ragdoll,
who wasn't very good.

Jo found a story
about bad ghosts
who tricked
children and
good ghosts
who saved them.

Jess tried on all
the possible
clothes she
could wear to
their birthday party.

She had just
decided on a tartan skirt,
a sleeveless top and her new joggers
when they heard their mum's voice.

"Five more minutes, you lot! Then lunch will be ready and I'll be in to check."

The three girls looked at each other.

Amy scooped all the toys into a big pile and pushed them under her bed.

Jo gathered up all the books and plonked them onto the bottom shelf of the bookcase.

Jess grabbed the clothes from all over the floor and shoved them into the bottom of the wardrobe.

The bedroom door opened.

"Well done," said Mum. She looked around. "Should I check to see if everything is in its right place?"

"No need to," said Jess. "We've done it perfectly."

"Everything is fine, Mum," said Jo.

"We did it all just the way you like us to," said Amy.

"Good," said Mum. She placed three piles of money on top of the cupboard. "After lunch I want you all in the back yard to clean up the mess of toys there too. And this time, I'm going to help."

Birthday Shopping

On Saturday morning, after breakfast, Dad handed each of the girls a little more money.

"You did a good job," he said. "Tidying the yard."

"I have an idea," said Mum. "Why don't you each buy for just one sister. So Amy buy for Jo, Jo buy for Jess and Jess buy for Amy. That would be simpler."

The girls shook their heads.

"I have
to get presents
for both my sisters,"
said Amy.

"Me too," said Jo.

"And me,"
said Jess.

So Amy went to the
main street with Mum.
Jo went with Dad to the
shopping centre.

Jess and Aunty Jen
headed for the
markets.

Amy and Mum
walked past a bookshop.
"You could buy them
books," said Mum.
Amy shook her head.
They went past the pet shop.
"I could buy them fish," said Amy.
Mum shook her head.

Then they reached the toy shop.
They went up and down
the different aisles.

They walked past iPods and Game
Boys.

"Too expensive," said Mum.

They looked at pencils and puzzles.

"Too boring," said Amy.

She went down the last aisle
by herself. Then she came running
back to her mum.
"I love these,"
she said.

Amy held
up a plastic
sword and
a shield.
"These are
just right."

Jo and Dad went through the big
doors of the shopping
centre and
took the
escalator
up to
the shops.

They passed a clothes shop.
"You could buy them funny
hats," said Dad.
Jo shook
her head.

They went past a cake shop.
"I could buy them
a chocolate cake each," said Jo.
Dad shook his head.

Then they reached
the variety shop. They saw
cricket sets and tennis racquets.

"Too expensive," said Dad.

They looked
at bangles
and bracelets.

"Too boring,"
said Jo.

She went off to the back corner
of the shop where there was a special
display of magical hats and cloaks,
model castles and mystery posters.

37

Jo came back with
a black and silver
wand and a book
of magic spells.
"Perfect," she said.
"These will be fantastic."

Jess and Aunty Jen walked into the
grounds of the church market. They
bought ice creams and watched
a clown, a fire-eater and a man
dressed as a statue that
never moved.

They passed
a gardening stall.
"What about these plants?"
Aunty Jen pointed to some pots.
"It says they eat flies."
Jess shook
her head.

They stopped near a toy stall.
"I could get them each a big
stuffed toy gorilla?"
Aunty Jen shook her head.

They went further into the market
where there were stalls with silver and
gold jewellery.

"Too expensive," said Aunty Jen.

They stopped in front
of a basket of
garden gnomes.

"Too boring,"
said Jess.

42

She moved to a new stall of fancy-dress clothes. There were turbans and scarves and flowing cloaks. She tried on a sparkling silver crown and a ring with a giant red stone in the centre.

"Perfect," said Jess.
"Just what I want."

Back at the house, each of
the girls held tightly to her shopping.
"You'll never guess what
I bought you," Jo grinned at her sisters.
"I got you the *best* presents," said Jess.
"Me too," said Amy.

The Birthday Party

It was the night before the girls' birthday.

In the lounge room Amy was wrapping the sword for Jo and the shield for Jess. In the dining room, Jo was wrapping the wand for Jess and the book of spells for Amy. In the bedroom Jess was wrapping the crown for Amy and the ring for Jo.

They placed the presents on the coffee table and went into the kitchen.

Mum was icing three separate cakes:
chocolate for Amy, lemon for Jo and
orange for Jess. Each girl got to dip
a finger into the icing bowl. It tasted
good. Dad was making chocolate
crackles and Aunty Jen was filling
little bags with lollies – one
for each person
at the party.

"Time for bed," said Mum as she
put all the bowls into the sink.

"It's too early," said Jo.

"There's still things to do," said Amy.

"We're not tired," said Jess.

"BED!" said Mum.

They tossed and they turned.
They giggled and they chatted.
They got up to get drinks of water.
Finally Dad came
into the bedroom.

"If you girls don't lie down and go to sleep, there'll be no party tomorrow."

They were quiet then. Each one slowly fell asleep, dreaming of presents, parties and birthday cake.

"Happy Birthday,
Happy Birthday,
Happy Birthday,"

said Mum next morning.
"Breakfast first and then presents."

Dad served them fruit salad with strawberries and pineapple, bananas and mango. "Special breakfast for special six-year-olds," he said.

He wiped the last sticky bit of mango from Amy's face. "And now it's time for presents."

The whole family sat on the floor in the lounge room. First there was a box that had come in the mail from Grandma. "I bet it's books," said Jo. And it was.

Then they opened a present of CDs from Uncle John, board games from Mum and Dad and puzzles from Aunty Jen.

"These are for you." Amy passed her gifts to Jo and Jess.

"And for you." Jo passed her presents to her sisters.

Jess did the same.

There was
poking and prodding,
feeling each present
and trying to guess
what it was.

Paper and ribbon
was ripped from
each parcel.

Silence.
Then, "Thank you,"
they each said.

Amy watched as the sword and
shield were put back down on the floor.
Jo watched as the wand and the book
of spells were placed back in the
pile of paper and Jess watched
as the crown and the ring lay
under a chair.

After a few minutes,
Amy reached over and picked up
the sword and shield. "These are really
good to play with," she said. "You can
be really brave."

Jo pushed the pile of paper aside and took the wand and the magic book. "You can play at being magicians with these," she said. "You can make spells and do tricks."

Jess put on the crown and the ring. "I must be a princess," she said. She pointed to Jo. "You are my special magician who has to make up magic spells and trick my enemies.

And you, Amy, must be the warrior
who will protect us from the
wicked soldiers who
are coming to
steal all our
presents."

Mum, Dad
and Aunty Jen
gathered up the
wrapping paper and
slipped quietly out of the room.

In the afternoon, lots of friends from
school came to the birthday party.

They played pass the parcel,
pin the tail on the donkey and
musical chairs. They hunted
for treasure all around
the garden.

They ate fairy bread and sausage rolls
and all of Dad's chocolate crackles.
Three lots of candles were lit and then
blown out, the birthday cakes were cut
and everyone sang "Happy Birthday"
three times.

Finally, the last balloon had burst and the last guest had gone, clutching a lolly bag. The princess, the magician and the warrior agreed it was the best birthday they had ever had.